# IMPROVE YOUR
# SWIMMING
# & DIVING
# SKILLS

**Emma Fischel**

Consultant: **John Verrier**
(Amateur Swimming Association)

Additional advice: **Doug Campbell**
(Barnet Copthall Swimming Pool)

Designed by **Chris Scollen**

Additional designs by **Adrienne Kern**

Illustrated by **Tessa Land, Joe McEwan**
and **Chris Lyon**

All photographs courtesy of **All-sport UK**

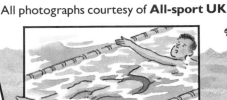

With thanks to **Barnet Copthall Swimming Pool,
Lisa Graham, Ben Price** and **Jason Statham**

This book was produced in association with SPEEDO®

# Contents

First published in 1989 by
Usborne Publishing Ltd.,
20 Garrick Street, London WC2E 9BJ,
England. Copyright © 1989
Usborne Publishing Ltd.

Printed in Belgium.

# Using this book

**Tips throughout the book help you develop your style and point out common mistakes to avoid.**

**Short, regular exercise is better than occasional long sessions.**

To swim well you need a good stroke style. The first part of this book has step-by-step diagrams to help you build up your technique. Try to memorize the positions before you swim but don't worry if you can't follow them exactly – you may need to adapt them slightly to suit you.

**Using a float helps you practise part of a stroke.**

Getting fitter helps you swim faster and longer. It is best to combine swimming with land exercises such as the ones in this book. The book also explains what happens to your body when you exercise. This helps you plan sessions to get the most from them.

| Warm up | ✓ | ✓ |
| Endurance | ✓ | ✓ |
| Drills | ✓ | ✓ |
| Main set | ✓ | ✓ |
| Speed | ✓ | |

A good way to test your skills and meet other keen swimmers is by entering competitions. For this, you need to plan your training carefully. At the back of the book there is a sample training session, with target times you can monitor your progress by.

Your mental attitude can make all the difference to your competition results. In this book you can see how to approach a race in a confident – and winning – frame of mind. There are also tips on how to hit competitions at your mental and physical peak.

If you are interested in diving, you can use this book to give you a good basic grounding, before going further with the help of a qualified coach. There is advice on using a springboard and examples of the kinds of dive you might see at top competition level. You can also find out about Olympic diving, and how it is organized and judged.

**Try not to rush your diving progress. You can easily lose confidence or even injure yourself.**

## Warning

Whether you swim or dive, basic safety knowledge is essential. There are tips throughout the book on situations to avoid, with advice on what to do if you are in difficulty or need to go to the help of someone else.

# About swimming

Below you can see how people float and move through water. Understanding how these affect your swimming helps you see why developing a good stroke technique is so important.

## Floating in water

Whether an object floats or sinks depends on its density (how heavy it is in relation to its size). If two objects are the same size but one is heavier, its density is higher. Something less dense than water floats, while something denser than water sinks.

**Human density is slightly less than water density, so people float but with most of their body underwater.**

**The air in your lungs also helps you float.**

**You float more easily in the sea because salt water has a slightly higher density.**

**Bone and muscle sink but fatty tissue floats, so someone with more fat finds floating easier.**

**People with heavy bones and large muscles may find the way they float makes swimming harder.**

## Test your buoyancy

To see how well you float, first curl up into a ball, face down in the water, then hold your knees and see where you float in the water. This is called a mushroom float.

**The angle you float at depends on how your bone, muscle and fat are distributed.**

Most people float horizontally, or almost so, which gives them a comfortable position for swimming.

## Moving through water

Walking through water is harder than walking on land because as you push forwards the water pushes back against you. This is called water resistance.

Water resistance also happens when you swim and is increased by waves which build up round your body, slowing you down even more.

**Water parts as you swim, forming waves to your front, sides and behind you.**

**Your feet leave a 'hole' as you move. It is immediately filled by swirling water.**

**A wall of water called a bow wave forms in front of you. It gets bigger the higher your head is and the faster you swim.**

**A good swimming style reduces the problem of water resistance.**

# Water safety

Taking the safety measures outlined below will help you get the most enjoyment out of swimming, whether it is in a pool or open water.

## Pool safety

★ Don't run around the pool edge: you could slip over or fall in.
★ If you jump in, check first that there are no swimmers around.
★ It is dangerous to duck people and can destroy their confidence.
★ Try to be thoughtful about other swimmers. You can easily collide if you don't look where you are going.
★ If you are allowed to use equipment, be careful with it. Flippers can hurt someone if you run into them; snorkels can make you lose your sense of direction and you could swim under the diving area.

## Swimming in rivers and the sea

If you swim anywhere other than in a pool make sure you go with someone else. If you have any doubts about whether it is safe, don't swim.

Stay clear of boats. They take time to change direction and you may not even be seen.

Note where lifebelts or other emergency aids are kept.

Don't swim near piers or breakwaters. Currents and waves around them can be too strong even for very good swimmers.

Swim parallel to the shore. If you swim out to sea you may get too tired to swim back.

Never swim straight after a meal. Allow yourself about an hour to digest your food.

Check whether the tide is going out or coming in.

Open water is usually much colder than in a pool, so you won't be able to swim as far.

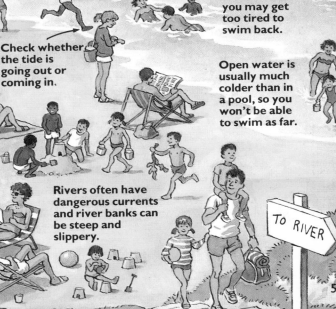

If notices or flags show you where to swim, follow their advice. Never swim if danger flags are flying.

Rivers often have dangerous currents and river banks can be steep and slippery.

TO RIVER

# Getting started

Whichever stroke you swim, you need to consider the same five things: your body position, leg action, arm action, breathing and timing. Below are some general points which relate to every stroke.

Your body position affects the whole stroke, so you need to get it right first of all. Aim to stay as streamlined as you possibly can.

How your head lies in the water has a strong effect on your body position.

Your leg kick helps hold your body in a good position. You need to kick strongly to stay as horizontal as possible.

Many style problems are caused by breathing at the wrong time. Try not to let your breathing interrupt the leg and arm action.

To keep streamlined, it may help to imagine you are swimming through a narrow tunnel.

Timing is the way all the stages fit together to form the complete stroke.

Most of the power in a stroke comes from your arms* but they can only work properly if your body position is right.

Sty
ti

## All strokes

★ To develop your all-round ability, it is a good idea to practise all the strokes equally, even if you have a particular favourite. You can always concentrate on one stroke later on and you may find that, as your skills improve, your stroke preferences change.
★ At first, try to improve your distance rather than your speed. This gives you more time to think about your technique, and also builds up your stamina.
★ Try to make your stroke action smooth; jerky swimming slows you down.
★ Aim to cut through the water like a spear as you swim, without moving your arms and legs too far sideways or down.
★ Remember that no two people swim a stroke exactly the same way. You may want to adapt some actions slightly to suit your physical ability and personal style.

*In breaststroke most of the power comes from your legs.

# Using your hands

The way you use your hands makes a lot of difference to how well you swim. For maximum efficiency, you need to keep changing their angle during the arm action. To understand when and why you do this it helps to divide the action into five stages. Below you can see what happens at each stage.*

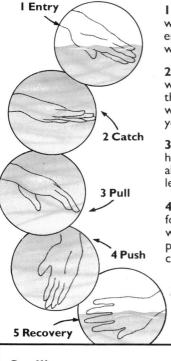

**I Entry**

**2 Catch**

**3 Pull**

**4 Push**

**5 Recovery**

1 Slice your hand into the water at an angle so that it enters smoothly and without splashing.

2 Begin to press against the water instead of slicing through it, so you use water resistance to propel you forwards.

3 Reach forwards with your hand and pull your body along until your hand is level with your shoulder.

4 To continue moving forwards, push against the water until your hand is past the lower line of your costume.

5 Bring your hand cleanly out of the water to recover on the surface.

## Underwater confidence

Skills and drills

Most strokes involve putting your face under the water at some stage. Below you can see how to practise doing this, and learn how to control your breathing.

**It helps if you try not to wipe your eyes or shake your head when you surface.**

To get used to your face being underwater, bend forwards and put your mouth underwater, then straighten up. Repeat with more of your face underwater each time until you can submerge it completely, keeping your eyes open.

**Stop if you feel any strain.**

Good swimmers use 'explosive breathing' to force air in and out of their lungs.

Breathe in, then put your head underwater and breathe out. Lift your head out and breathe in. Keep repeating this, breathing in as quickly as you can and breathing out hard through your mouth.

## Sculling

Skills and drills

Finding the best hand action for a stroke involves getting the 'feel' of the water. A good way to learn how water reacts to your hand movements is by sculling.

Stand with your shoulders and hands just underwater. Press your hands smoothly outwards, little fingers on top, then inwards, thumbs uppermost.

**You should see 'holes' appear in the water above your hands.**

*These pictures show the frontcrawl hand movements, but the principle remains the same for all strokes.*

# Frontcrawl

Frontcrawl is the fastest of all the strokes. In freestyle races, where you can choose the stroke you swim, nearly all swimmers use frontcrawl. It is a natural stroke to progress to from dog-paddle but to swim it really well takes a lot of practice.

## Before you start

How smooth and fast your frontcrawl is depends as much on how you lie in the water as on your stroke action. This picture shows the ideal body position to aim for.

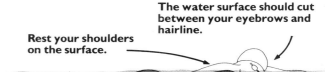

**The water surface should cut between your eyebrows and hairline.**

**Rest your shoulders on the surface.**

**Keep your hips just under the surface.**

**Point your nose forwards and down.**

## The stroke

Slide your right arm forwards into the water with your elbow high. Slice your hand in in front of your shoulder.

Begin to bend your right elbow as you brush your left thumb against your thigh below the line of your costume.

Lift your left arm out of the water by bending your elbow. Bend your right arm down and back, keeping the elbow high.

While your left arm recovers, move your right arm down and back to below your shoulder, with your elbow bent up to 90°.

Slide your left arm forwards into the water as you push your right arm back towards your hip.

Lift your right arm out of the water, elbow first, and start to press your left arm down.

## Leg kicks

★ Practise the kick holding on to the rail before you try the whole stroke.
★ Kicking from your hips, not your knees, gives you more power. Use a whip-like action to kick up and try to kick without pausing.
★ Don't bend your knees too much. You should find they bend the right amount naturally if you keep your legs close together and relaxed.
★ Try to relax your ankles and turn your feet inwards, if you can.
★ Don't do more than just break the surface with your feet.

## Stroke cycles

The number of times you kick while you complete both armstrokes is your stroke cycle. You can use a six-beat cycle (six kicks to the action of both arms) or, if you prefer, a two- or four-beat cycle.

Try experimenting to see which cycle suits you. When you are happy with your leg kick, let your arms join in naturally. As your arm enters the water, kick your opposite leg upwards to start the cycle.

A six-beat cycle is the most popular for frontcrawl as it is powerful and keeps your body streamlined. In long races many swimmers use a less tiring two-beat kick, sometimes changing to six for a final spurt.

## Breathing

In frontcrawl, you can breathe either to the left or the right every complete arm cycle. As your arm leaves the water, your shoulder lifts up naturally and helps you turn your head to that side to breathe. Breathe out forcibly through your mouth, then breathe in as quickly as possible before returning your face to the water.

## Timing

**This swimmer is breathing to the left.**

**Top swimmers take about one-fifth of a second to complete the whole breathing sequence.**

Many competitive swimmers breathe alternately to the left and right at every third armstroke. This is known as bilateral breathing. It is good for seeing where the opposition is in a race and also keeps your body flatter in the water.

To practise breathing without upsetting your stroke rhythm, hold a float and start kicking. Place your face in the water, then lift it up to breathe out and in. Kick as evenly as you can as you do so.

9

# Breaststroke

Breaststroke was the first stroke to be swum competitively. It can also be a life-saver: most people swim a form of it if they are in difficulty.

## The stroke

Glide with your legs straight, your arms extended and pressed against your ears, and your face in the water.

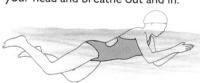

Sweep your hands out, back and down but keep them in front of your shoulders. Lift your head and breathe out and in.

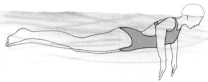

Sweep your hands down, palms pitched thumbs down, and with your elbows bent and kept high. Keep your legs straight.

Sweep your hands in, palms facing each other, to below your chin. Bend your knees so your heels rise upwards.

As you push your hands forwards, turn your feet out and sweep them out and back in an accelerating whip-like action.

If it suits you, hold this stretched, streamlined position for a glide before starting again with the arm action.

## Arm and leg actions

Two common mistakes are sweeping your arms and legs out sideways and flat, and doing the arm and leg actions at the same time.

The diagrams on the right show the correct movements your arms and legs should make. Practise them separately* until they become automatic, then you can concentrate on timing them correctly when you swim the whole stroke.

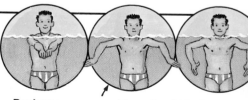

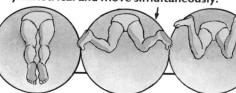

**Both your arms and legs should look symmetrical and move simultaneously.**

*Stand in shoulder-deep water to practise the arms; hold a float while you practise the legs.

# Foot position

Unlike the other strokes, most of the power in breaststroke comes from your legs. If your feet are at the correct angles your kick will be much stronger, although the positions are not easy for most people and need practice. Try the positions below once you feel happy with the movement and timing of your arm and leg actions.

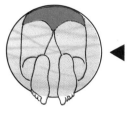

Turn the soles of your feet up at the start of the leg action.

Lift your heels up towards the surface, keeping them inside the width of your hips, if you can.

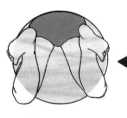

Rotate your ankles so your feet turn out as the kick begins.

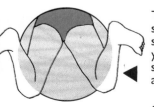

Turn your feet so they are sideways as your legs sweep out and down.

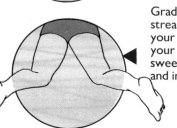

Gradually streamline your feet as your legs sweep down and in.

Skills and drills

## Kick check

Lie on your back, holding a float under each arm to keep you stable. Practise the kick, watching to see that your legs are doing the right movements.

**Make sure your legs work in unison.**

## Co-ordination

Extend your arms out in front of you. Do two breaststroke leg kicks, followed by one arm action. Then kick three times, followed by another arm action. Repeat the sequence a few times.

**Try not to rush the changeover from the leg to arm action.**

Style tips

## Stroke action

★ Keep your body as flat as you can and try to make as little movement as possible when you lift your head to breathe.
★ Don't pull your arms beyond your shoulder line. If you pull too early you weaken the power of your kick.
★ Make sure that your palms face out, then back, then finally in as your arm movement accelerates. Use more of a swirling than a pressing action.
★ Don't let your feet break the surface when you kick.

# Backstroke

Backstroke is the name for any stroke swum on the back. The most popular is backcrawl, which is used by competitive swimmers.

When you swim on your back, always check before you start that there is no danger of colliding with other swimmers.

## The backcrawl stroke

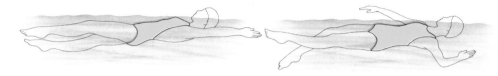

Slide your left hand into the water with your arm straight. Place your right arm straight alongside your body, thumb up.

Press your left arm down and outwards in a circular path as you lift your right arm out of the water.

Sweep your left arm towards your thigh, with your elbow bending most when your hand, elbow and shoulder are in line.

Straighten your left arm as you sweep it towards your thigh, ending with a strong down-push.

## Stroke action

**Style tips**

★ Rest your head as if it were on a pillow, with your chin tucked slightly into your neck. Look up and back down the pool.
★ Try to keep your elbow high during the stroke.
★ Enter your hand smoothly, little finger first, with the minimum splashing.
★ Kick up and down from your hips, using a six-beat stroke cycle. Try not to use a cycling action; it is much weaker and your knees will break the surface.
★ Kick up with a whip-like action, keeping your feet relaxed and turned slightly inwards. Don't let them break the surface.

## Breathing

Breathing in backcrawl is fairly relaxed. Breathe out as one arm enters the water and in as the other enters. Open your mouth wide when you breathe.

Force the air in and out so your body gets sufficient oxygen (see page 25).

## Body roll

As your arm reaches back into the water your body naturally rolls sideways. This body roll makes the underwater arm action easier, but try to avoid rolling too much or moving sideways as this slows you down.

You can use the ways shown below to control the amount your body rolls.

> Keep your head still. If you move it your body may roll too much.

> Kick strongly to keep your body in a good position and balance the arm action.

## Leg action

> Skills and drills

To get used to kicking with your body at an angle, roll to one side as shown in the picture. Kick six times then roll on to the opposite side. Reverse your arm positions and kick six times, then roll back and repeat the sequence.

## Arm action

Hold a float to your chest with one arm and concentrate on using your free arm well. Swap the float round and practise with the other arm.

## Arm entry

Entering your arm into the water at the wrong angle weakens your stroke. If you enter your arm 'over-centre' it reaches too far across your body and may make your hips move outwards. Entering your arm 'wide' means it reaches out too far sideways from your body, giving your arm action less power.

Use the tips below to help you get the correct arm angle.

> Enter your arm into the water in line with its own shoulder.

> Brush your ear with your arm as it enters the water.

> Imagine a line running down the middle of your body and don't let your arm cross it.

13

# Butterfly

Butterfly is a very graceful stroke when it is swum really well and is second in speed to frontcrawl. In 1952 it became the fourth stroke to be recognized in competitive swimming events.

## The stroke

Enter your arms into the water in line with your shoulders, with your hands pitched thumbs down.

Sweep your hands downwards and outwards, bending your elbows and making sure you keep them high.

Now push both of your hands towards each other underneath your chest, then accelerate them backwards towards your feet.

Bring your arms elbow-first out of the water and swing them smoothly forwards, little fingers uppermost. Push your chin forwards and take a quick breath.

## Leg kick

Your legs work together, kicking down once as your hands enter the water, then again when they leave it. You will probably find this happens naturally.

At the beginning of the kick, bend your knees to about 90°. Start kicking from your hips, accelerating through your knees, which you should straighten as you kick. Try to keep your feet relaxed.

As butterfly is quite strenuous, practise over a short distance, say five metres, to start with. This way you can concentrate on building up the rhythm without tiring yourself.

**The first kick is more important. Unless you kick strongly, your body moves downwards too much as your arms leave the water.**

**The second kick keeps you steady while your arms finish the underwater action.**

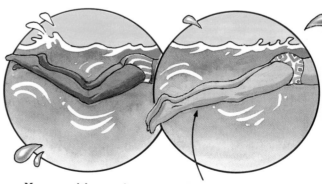

**You can either make your first kick stronger, or kick equally both times.**

**To kick both legs in unison it helps to imagine they are tied together.***

*Never actually try this – it is for imagination only.*

# Body movement

Your arm and leg movements make your hips move up and down, so you undulate like a wave. Too much or too little undulation weakens your stroke.

Below are some of the things to watch out for if you find yourself having problems with the body movement.

**Kicking too deep makes your hips shoot to the surface and your legs drop down further.**

**Lifting your head too high when you breathe makes your hips drop and your legs rise.**

**Pausing after your arms enter the water disturbs the rhythm of your body movement.**

**Keeping your head up as your arms enter the water stops your body and arms moving properly.**

Skills and drills

## Co-ordination

**Use a float to help you.**

One-arm butterfly is a good way to practise timing the stroke. Using the butterfly kick, swim one width with just the right arm doing the stroke, then another using just the left arm.

Style tips

## Arm action

★ As your arms provide most of the power, mobile shoulders and a strong upper body will improve your stroke. See pages 34-35 for exercises.

★ Try to keep your shoulders level with the water and concentrate on making both arms work together. They should enter the water in line with your shoulders, with your elbows higher than your hands.

★ Make sure your arms clear the surface as they recover.

## Leg action

★ Try to kick smoothly.

★ If you find your hips drop, eventually forcing you to stop, try practising the leg kick on its own for a while.

## Breathing

Start raising your head and shoulders when your arms are underwater, level with your chest. Stretch your neck as your arms leave the water, lifting your head until your chin just clears the surface. Breathe out forcibly through your mouth, then breathe in immediately.

**Keep your head straight, not to one side, or your shoulders will drop.**

15

# Diving

Top divers make diving look graceful and effortless, but they need total co-ordination, perfect balance and strength to achieve this. Diving can be dangerous if you don't have expert guidance, so for anything beyond the dives shown here you should get the help of a qualified coach.*

Before you try out any of the dives on these pages, make sure you read the safety tips below.

## Before you start

You need to feel confident about swimming and turning underwater with your eyes open before you start diving.

Take a deep breath, then go underwater. Resurface before you strain for breath.

Push off from the wall and glide through a hoop or a partner's legs.

Try picking up coins from the bottom of the pool, or walking on your hands.

## Jumping

Every standing dive is based on a confident jump. Trying the jumps below will help as, to give yourself time to do them, you need to make a good, high take-off.

### Star jump

Jump up and out, making a star shape with your arms and legs. Before you hit the water, try to put your arms by your sides and bring your legs together, so you are as straight and vertical as possible.

### Tuck jump

Jump up and out with your arms by your sides. At the top of your jump, tuck your knees up and clasp them with your hands. Straighten to as near vertical as you can before hitting the water.

## Diving safety

★ Only dive in a pool. You can easily misjudge the depth of a river or the sea.
★ Always check that the water is deep enough. It should be at least 1.5m deep for the dives on these pages. Most pools are marked at the sides to tell you their depth.
★ Never play around in a diving area and always check that there are no swimmers around when you dive.
★ Take it slowly. The dives shown here get gradually more difficult – only move from one to the next when you feel fully confident.
★ If you have a cold or earache, seek your doctor's advice before you do any diving.

*Try your local pool or library for details of diving clubs or classes in your area.

# Starting to dive

In the dives below, aim for a clean entry into the water, followed by a shallow glide. Don't try to go deep on your dive; make sure the water depth is at least 1.5m.

## Sitting dive

**I** Sit on the poolside, with your weight well forwards and your feet on the bar. Point your arms at the pool, one hand clasping the other, with your head tucked between your arms.

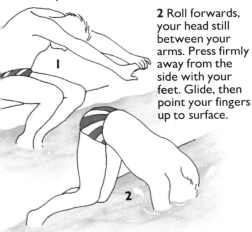

**2** Roll forwards, your head still between your arms. Press firmly away from the side with your feet. Glide, then point your fingers up to surface.

> ## Streamlined diving
>
> **Style tips**
>
> ★ Before you put your head down to dive, decide where you want to enter the water. Fix on a point that feels right for you, not too far out but not too close to the poolside.
> ★ Press your arms against your ears and make sure one hand is clasping the other when you dive.
> ★ Keep your feet stretched hard from the moment you leave the poolside until you resurface.
> ★ Point your hands down as you enter the water; your body will follow them naturally.
> ★ When you want to resurface, point your fingers upwards.

## The lunge

**I** Start from the position shown, with your body bent forwards from your hips. Hold your arms straight and pointing at the water, with your head between them.

**2** Bend further forwards and, as you overbalance, push off hard from your leading foot. Bring your legs together before they enter the water.

## Kneeling dive

**I** Kneel on one knee, gripping the pool edge with your other foot. Raise your arms, one hand clasping the other, with your head between your arms.

**2** Bend forwards and as you overbalance, push off with your left foot, keeping your body stretched. Bring your legs together in the air.

**Glide with your arms straight ahead until you resurface.**

**As you improve, bend less and less until you are almost upright.**

# The plunge

The plunge is the most difficult dive you should attempt without expert help. It forms the basis of the racing start on page 20.

**1** Stand with your feet about hip-width apart, your toes curled round the pool edge. Bend your knees and hips slightly, with your weight pushed forwards and your head and neck continuing the natural curve of your spine.

**2** Swing your arms forwards so your body starts to follow them and your knees begin to bend. Push off hard from the poolside with a strong drive from your legs.

**3** As your feet leave the side, try to straighten your body. Keep your legs streamlined, feet together and toes pointed.

**4** Enter the water fingers first. When your feet are underwater, lift your head and point your hands upwards to move smoothly to the surface.

**Practise the plunge in at least 1.5m of water.**

I

2

3

4

## The perfect plunge

★ Swing your arms strongly to get the maximum power you can into the dive.
★ Try to make your feet go through the same 'hole' in the water as your hands.
★ Keep your body firm and streamlined during th underwater glide; if yc relax it you lose spee

**Keep you hands together, in line wi your hea**

**Point your arms forwards and down.**

## Gliding underwater

To practise your glide, push off strongly from the wall of the pool. Concentrate on keeping your body streamlined as you glide and return to the surface as smoothly as possible. Get a friend to measure how far you glide as you improve.

*Skills and drills*

## Belly flops

A belly flop happens if you hold your head too high when you take off. Your body smacks down flat on the water instead of entering it at a smooth angle. To avoid belly flops, tuck your head towards your chest as you dive.

Most belly flops are caused by trying a difficult dive before mastering the easier ones properly.

# Using the springboard

If you are interested in board diving, the first thing to do is learn to use the springboard well. Try the jumps below on a 1m springboard.*

## Standing jump

**1** Stand as straight as you can, with your feet as close together as feels comfortable.

**Grip the edge of the board with your toes.**

**2** Move your arms up and sideways. As your hands pass your shoulders, stand on your toes. The board will move up slightly.

**Move your arms to your sides after you jump.**

**3** Bend your knees and bring your arms down to your hips. Stay crouched as the board goes down until you feel it can go no lower.

**4** At the board's lowest, move your arms up in a 'Y' shape, stretch your knees and point your toes as you jump.

## Running jump

**1** Walk three or four steps, making the last a little longer and faster.

**2** As you take the last step, bend up your trailing knee and swing your arms up.

**Pace out the steps first so you know how far back to stand on the board.**

**3** As you leave the board, keep your head still but look for the end of the board. At the top of the jump begin to straighten your left leg so both feet meet the board together.

**4** As you land, move your arms down and out. As the board continues downwards, start swinging your arms forwards.

**5** Bring your arms up in a 'Y' shape. Push off strongly from the board as it goes up.

**6** While in the air, bring your arms down to your sides. Enter the water as near vertical as possible.

*Only try diving from a springboard with the help of a qualified coach.*

## Springboard safety

★ The height and springiness of a board take getting used to, so it is a good idea to practise all the movements on land first or, if you can, on a trampoline.
★ Always check that there are no swimmers around the springboard when you jump.

## Springboard style

★ Try to go with the natural movement of the board: after jumping upwards land softly on it, pushing it down rather than stamping on it.
★ Don't jump away from the board, but let its springiness propel you off.
★ Make sure you adjust the springboard to suit you (see page 41).

# Racing starts and finishes

On the next eight pages you can find out about the skills needed for competitive swimming. Races are often won by narrow margins and developing a strong start and finish can save you vital seconds.

## The grab start

This is the most popular forward start. Using your hands as well as your feet gives your take-off extra power.

**1** Bend your knees, with your feet hip-width apart and your toes curled round the block. Hold the block with your hands, either between or outside your feet, with your arms nearly straight. Keep your hips as far forwards as you can. At the signal,* pull hard on the block.

**2** As you overbalance, drop your knees and push your arms forwards. Raise your head and look forwards and down the pool. When your knees are nearly level with your feet, push off hard from the block, extending your legs so you move up and outwards.

**Your head and neck should follow the natural curve of your spine.**

**Just listen for the starting signal; you don't have to look.**

### The underwater glide

★ Try to make your glide as long as possible. It is faster than surface swimming as there are less waves to slow you down.
★ Keep streamlined as you glide; don't relax your body.
★ Start kicking as you slow to near swimming speed and begin the underwater arm action in preparation for breaking the surface.
★ Try to go smoothly into your first surface stroke, without a pause.

**Skills and drills**

### Knee tucks

Knee tucks build up strength in your legs so you can push off powerfully.
    Jump up and tuck your knees into your chest, straightening up before you land. Try ten jumps, followed by a rest, then complete two more sets of ten jumps.

**3** After you leave the block, lower your head to keep streamlined. Either bend slightly at the highest point of the dive and enter the water at quite a deep angle or, if it suits you more, keep your body straight in flight for a shallower entry.

**Practise the grab start in water at least 1.5m deep.**

**4** On entry, try to keep as streamlined as possible, with your hands close together and fingers pointed. Keep your head between your arms and your ankles stretched. As you glide, stretch your hands forwards and up, one on top of the other.

*See page 39 for starting signals and false starts.

# The backcrawl start

**I** Hold the backcrawl bar and, if it suits you, put one foot slightly higher than the other. On 'Take your marks', pull yourself up into a crouched position, your head tucked down and elbows flexed.

**2** Push strongly on the bar to start yourself moving backwards. Push with your feet so your bottom rises clear of the water. As you leave the wall, throw your head up and back and move your arms up and outwards until they are extended beyond your head.

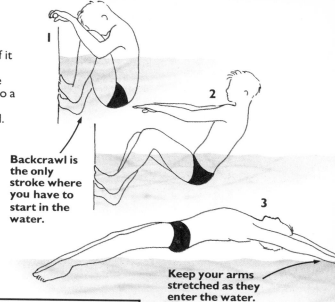

**Backcrawl is the only stroke where you have to start in the water.**

**Keep your arms stretched as they enter the water.**

## Finishing a race

Finishing a race often relies on split-second judgement. You may have to decide very quickly whether to start a new armstroke or lengthen the current one.

As you approach the wall, speed up by kicking hard, then jab your arm towards it.

In breaststroke and butterfly both hands should touch the wall together; in frontcrawl and backcrawl you can make the touch with one hand.

**3** As your hands enter the water, keep arching your back so your legs remain clear of the water for as long as possible. Glide with your arms extended and your hands stretched out, one on top of the other. Start kicking hard as you slow down. Try to go smoothly into the stroke as you surface.

**It takes practice to judge your distance from the wall.**

**To save time, touch the wall with your fingertips rather than your palm.**

**Keep your face in the water; lifting your head shortens your arm reach.**

## Race tactics

**Style tips**

★ While you wait for the starting signal, block everything else out of your mind. Try not to think about the actual movements of the start; you react faster if you just concentrate on listening for the signal.

★ Keep kicking hard right to the finish. Relaxing as you get near the wall may lose you the race.

# Racing turns

Turning well takes practice, but can make quite a difference to your race results. Below are some of the most popular racing turns.

## Backcrawl spin turn

To help you judge your distance from the wall when you swim on your back, most pools have markers 5m from the pool ends. After you pass the marker and take your final armstroke, drop your head back. Touch the wall behind your head, with your fingers pointing out and down.

1 Quickly extend your arm, flex your legs and lift them out of the water with your feet and knees together.

**Scull with your free hand to speed up the spin.**

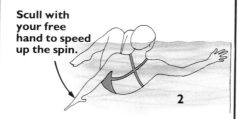

**2**

2 Swing your legs round towards the arm that touched the wall.

**You must surface within 10m of the turn.**

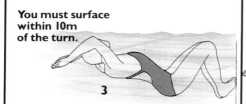

**3**

3 Bring your arms round beyond your head as your feet reach the wall. Push off strongly into the glide.

## Frontcrawl tumble turn

**Give a short butterfly-like kick with your legs.**

**1**

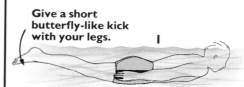

1 With one arm by your side, take your final armstroke. Pull the stroking arm back to your thigh, ready to start the turn.

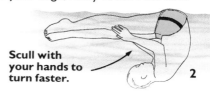

**Scull with your hands to turn faster.**

**2**

2 Drive your head underwater, moving downwards as fast as possible. Press your hands down towards the bottom of the pool. As you move down, tuck your legs up so they pass over your head on the surface.

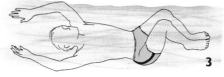

**3**

3 Push your head forwards as it turns to the surface. Stretch your legs until your feet touch the wall, then bend your knees slightly. Push off strongly with your arms flexed and your head between them.

**4**

4 Twist on to your front as you glide away and kick hard as you slow down. After about three kicks, press one hand down and out, ready to go into the stroke.

# Breaststroke turn

You can take one underwater stroke after the turn. As this is faster than surface swimming, make your turn deep enough to take advantage of it.

Try to time the approach so your arms are extended at the touch. Touch the wall with both hands simultaneously, keeping your shoulders horizontal.

**1** After the touch, flex your arms and lift your head so your body drops down.

**2** Bend your knees and move one hand away from the wall, palm up, towards your ribs. Move the other over the surface and slice it down into the water, followed by your head.

**Flex your hips and knees → to help you turn.**

**3** As you move round, extend your arms and bring your feet to the wall. Push off strongly.

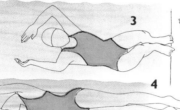

**4** As your glide slows down, pull your arms back to your thighs for the underwater stroke.

# Butterfly turn

The touch and push-off are very similar to those used in the breaststroke turn, but try to make the butterfly turn a bit shallower.

**1** Touch the wall with both hands at the same time. Keep your shoulders level as you touch.

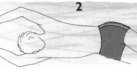

**2** Make sure you have turned to your front again before you take your first stroke. Kick for the surface and start the arm action as you reach it.

# Turning

**Style tips**

★ Try to take your final armstroke about one-and-a-half arms' lengths away from the wall.
★ Don't slow down as you approach the wall. Try to maintain full speed right up to the touch.
★ As you touch the wall, bend your arm then straighten it powerfully.*This gives extra momentum to the turn and makes it faster.
★ Try to move from the turn into the first stroke as smoothly as possible.

# Somersaulting

**Skills and drills**

Somersaulting is a good way to gain confidence about turning. Push off from the pool edge with your feet, then somersault underwater, keeping your eyes open as you do so.

*In frontcrawl you should do the same with your legs.*

# Individual medley

The individual medley is a big challenge as it combines four strokes in one race, over either 200m or 400m. It is particularly good if you have all-round ability and no specific best stroke.

## About the individual medley

Both the 200m and 400m medley need speed and stamina, but the 400m is a tough endurance race used in older age group swimming. In the 200m you swim 50m of each stroke; the 400m involves 100m of each stroke.

If you do have one strong stroke, make sure you don't neglect the others. It is just as important to practise your weakest and least favourite strokes. A solid performance on each stretch of the race is more likely to give good results.

### 200m medley order

| | | |
|---|---|---|
| First stroke: butterfly | 50m |
| Second stroke: backcrawl | 50m |
| Third stroke: breaststroke | 50m |
| Fourth stroke: freestyle | 50m |

Note: because you change from one stroke to another in a medley race, you need to use special turns. You can find out about how to turn at each changeover on page 26.

If you swim a medley race in a 25m pool, you use the normal turn for each stroke half-way through each 50m stretch.

## Pacing yourself

The medley is too long to swim at your fastest all the way through so you need to pace yourself. It is a good idea to work out some sort of plan beforehand. Base it on your own ability and stamina but keep it flexible: you should be prepared to change it in mid-race in response to competitors' actions.

**Sample race plan**

*Butterfly Swim fast, but not flat out. Try and relax into a smooth rhythm.*

*Backcrawl Start kicking harder, to keep high in the water. Don't forget to breathe out and in hard. Try to get as near the front as possible.*

*Breaststroke Change of rhythm from backcrawl - so don't rush the arm and leg actions. Try to go into the lead here.*

*Frontcrawl Swim as fast as possible. Keep face in the water for the last three strokes to the finish.*

The golden rule is never to start at full speed. This tires you out very quickly.

Try to balance your effort between the strokes, taking your strengths and weaknesses into account.

If you save your energy for one stroke you will fall behind on the others and be unable to catch up.

# How your body produces energy

When you swim, your muscles contract and relax. To do this they need energy, supplied by food. Your body uses two systems to convert food into energy, described on the right.

> The aerobic system needs a good supply of oxygen. It provides energy slowly and over a long time.

> The anaerobic system does not use oxygen. It supplies a limited amount of energy quickly.

## Stroke switching

Skills and drills

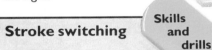

You need to adapt quickly to the new stroke at each changeover in a medley.
Try swimming 100m of one stroke followed by 100m of the next. This gives you time to think about the change of rhythm between the strokes.

As the medley is too long for the anaerobic system alone and too fast for the aerobic system, both are used at once.

### 'Oxygen debt'

Towards the end of a 200m medley, you will be swimming at a pace which requires more oxygen than you can take in. Lactic acid (a waste product from anaerobic exercise, only dealt with by oxygen) starts to build up in your muscles. This makes them feel heavy and hard to move.

The amount of oxygen you need to deal with the lactic acid created is known as your 'oxygen debt'.* A good training programme (see page 36) can minimize these effects and help you swim faster and for longer.

## Medley targets

To work out what speed to aim for on each stroke in a 200m medley, take your best time over 100m for each stroke, then halve it. Add between one and two seconds for a realistic medley time.

**This chart shows the percentage of the total time top swimmers take on each medley stroke.**

| Stroke | % 200m |
|---|---|
| Butterfly | 21.0 |
| Backcrawl | 25.0 |
| Breaststroke | 30.0 |
| Freestyle | 24.0 |

## Coping with race pressure

Style tips

★ Try not to look at other swimmers early in a race. It slows you down and you may panic, destroying your rhythm.
★ The pressure is greatest on your weakest stroke. It is a good idea to try simply to maintain your position here rather than forge ahead.
★ If you are behind try not to feel demoralized; concentrate on your swimming and not on the opposition. You can use the tips on pages 38-39 to help you get into the right frame of mind for a race.

*When you pant after a race, your body is replacing the oxygen it is 'owed'.

# Medley turns

Below are the most popular turns for the first and second stretches of a medley race. For the breaststroke to freestyle turn, follow the instructions for the breaststroke turn on page 23, but don't push off so deeply from the wall.

## First turn:
## butterfly to backcrawl

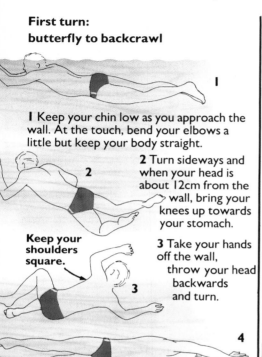

**1** Keep your chin low as you approach the wall. At the touch, bend your elbows a little but keep your body straight.

**2** Turn sideways and when your head is about 12cm from the wall, bring your knees up towards your stomach.

**Keep your shoulders square.**

**3** Take your hands off the wall, throw your head backwards and turn.

**4**

**4** Swing your hands up above your head as you push off strongly. Try to bounce off the wall, and keep your head steady.

## Second turn:
## backcrawl to breaststroke

**1** Reach for the wall and drop your head by looking back at the wall. As you touch, stop kicking and bend your knees up.

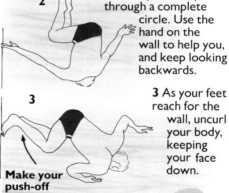

**2** Twist your body back through a complete circle. Use the hand on the wall to help you, and keep looking backwards.

**3** As your feet reach for the wall, uncurl your body, keeping your face down.

**Make your push-off deep.**

**Skills and drills**

## Muddled medleys

You can include all sorts of strange combinations of strokes and turns in your medley training. These are some ideas to start you off.

Use the arm action of one stroke and the legs of another. Use the turn that goes with the arm action.

Try swimming the medley in reverse order.

Swim a length of the backcrawl kick, then a length of the butterfly arms.

# Relays

In relays you swim as one of a team of four people, each swimming an equal distance. There are two relays, the freestyle and the medley.

## Wind-up start

**Starting position**

The first swimmer may use a grab start (see page 20) but take-over swimmers usually use a wind-up start. You build up momentum by swinging your arms. By stopping the arm movement as you dive your body is pushed forwards powerfully.

**The incoming swimmer must touch the wall before you leave the block.**

**1** When the incoming swimmer is about 5m away, move your arms up, out and forwards. Drop your head a little.

**Look forwards and down into the pool.**

**2** Swing your arms back past your shoulders in a circular movement and start to lift your head.

**3** Swing your hands round past your thighs, palms towards your legs. Extend your knees.

**4** As your arms swing below your body, keep them steady and push off hard from the block.

## Deciding the swimming order

The order of swimmers can have quite an effect on race results. Below are some of the things a coach takes into account when choosing the order.

*WHERE IS THE TOUGHEST OPPOSITION? WHO BREATHES ON THAT SIDE\* AND CAN WATCH THEM IN THE FINAL LENGTH?*

*WHO HAS THE BEST GRAB START AND SHOULD GO FIRST?*

*FASTEST FIRST?*

*SLOWEST FIRST?*

*TEMPERAMENT? WHO THRIVES ON A CLOSE FINISH? WHO PANICS?*

Often the best swimmers are wasted by being given too much catching up to do. Going first gives an early lead which encourages slower swimmers to perform well.

**With little difference in team members' speeds the slowest swimmer may lose some ground but the faster swimmers can make it up.**

### Timing the take-over

**Style tips**

★ Get into position when the incoming swimmer is about 20m away. Focus your attention on his or her head. Don't get drawn into starting early in the excitement of a close take-over.

★ Make sure you complete the arm swing properly, or your legs could enter the water first.

★ Try practising with your team members. One of you should practise as the incoming swimmer, another as the take-over swimmer. Ask the others to watch the timing.

*\*See page 9 for breathing sides.*

27

# Competitive diving

On these pages you can see the types of dive used in competitions. If you are interested in diving at this level you need to work with a qualified diving coach.* Many of the techniques are difficult to learn and they can be dangerous without proper supervision.

## About competitive diving

There are six main types of dive: forward, backward, reverse, inward, twist and armstand.** Each dive can be divided into three sections: take-off, flight and entry.

### Take-off

All dives take off either forwards, backwards or from an armstand.

**Reverse dives** take off forwards, but the diver turns in the air.

**Inward dives** take off backwards, and the diver enters the water facing away from the board.

### Flight

A diver can be straight, piked or tucked in flight.

**Tucked:** rolled into ball, bent hips and knees.

**Straight:** fully stretched, with no bending.

**Piked:** bent at hips, straight knees, fingertips touching toes.

### Entry

Dives can finish head or feet first, but the body must be straight and as near vertical as possible.

**Head first:** arms should be stretched above head in line with body.

**Feet first:** arms should be completely straight and close to body.

---

## Professional hints

*Style tips*

★ Top divers need strong ankles and legs to provide power for a good take-off, so they train regularly with weights.
★ Most divers practise on trampolines as well as diving boards. They sometimes use 'mini-tramps' on the poolside during practice. These give extra lift at the take-off.

## Diving champion

### Greg Louganis

Greg Louganis of the USA has won four Olympic gold medals. He gained more points in the 1984 and 1988 Olympics than any other diver has ever been awarded.

Many people consider him to be the best diver of all time.

*Try your local pool or library for information.
**In an armstand dive, instead of standing up, you stand on your arms before the take-off.

# Sample dives

There are six different groups of competitive dive, one on the highboard and five on the springboard. Below are two of the most difficult dives.

## Inward dive, piked

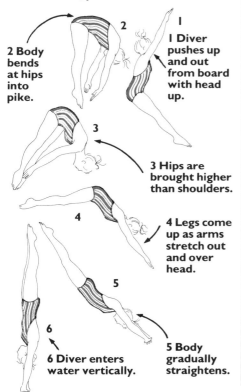

**2 Body bends at hips into pike.**

**1 Diver pushes up and out from board with head up.**

**3 Hips are brought higher than shoulders.**

**4 Legs come up as arms stretch out and over head.**

**5 Body gradually straightens.**

**6 Diver enters water vertically.**

## Forward dive, half twist

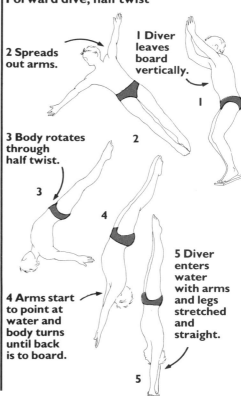

**2 Spreads out arms.**

**1 Diver leaves board vertically.**

**3 Body rotates through half twist.**

**4 Arms start to point at water and body turns until back is to board.**

**5 Diver enters water with arms and legs stretched and straight.**

## Judging

Major international competitions are supervised by a referee. Five or seven judges are positioned round the diving board. After each dive, the referee signals to the judges to award their marks. These marks are then recorded by two secretaries.

Competitors do a mixture of set dives and voluntary dives chosen from recognized groups.

Judges look for diving technique and ability, personal style and interpretation.

Dives are marked out of ten, with decimals to one place.

Marks are awarded either by pressing a button or holding cards up.

# Sychronized swimming

To try synchronized swimming (synchro), you need sculling ability* and a good sense of rhythm, as well as flexibility and stamina.

## About synchronized swimming

Synchro swimmers combine various strokes and arm and leg movements, set to music, to create patterns and shapes in the water. Solo swimmers synchronize with the music; group swimmers must also synchronize with each other.

## Competitions

There are solo, duet and team events, each with figure and routine sections. The figure section is made up of set movements. The routine section gives swimmers a chance to make up their own sequence and show their versatility.

**Small speakers under the surface allow swimmers to hear the music underwater.**

**In the past, one swimmer blew raspberries underwater to tell the others to change movement.**

**In the 'boost', one swimmer is propelled up and out of the water by the others.**

### Judging

Judges award points out of ten. Teams get an extra half point for every swimmer above four, as synchronization is harder. Touching the pool bottom loses a point.

Among other things, judges look for:
★ Good presentation and use of the pool.
★ How difficult the synchronization is.
★ Interpretation of the music.
★ Changes of mood and pace.

## Sample movements

Below are a solo and a team synchro movement you could try out.

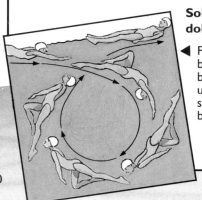

### Solo synchro: dolphin bent knee

◀ For this, you start bending your knee before it is underwater and straighten it as it breaks the surface.

### Team synchro: floating square ▲

Four people form a square. They scull with their free hands to move the square round.

*See page 7 for more about sculling.

# Water polo

Water polo is a fast and exciting game to play. Many pools have clubs or teams, and are willing to train beginners. Below you can see the basic skills required and you can also learn the main rules of the game.

## The main rules

There are two teams of up to eleven players each. Only seven of each team can be in the water at once. The aim is to score by putting the ball in the other team's goal.

There are four five-minute periods of play. The teams change ends between each period.

If the teams tie they have a five-minute break, then play for two three-minute periods.

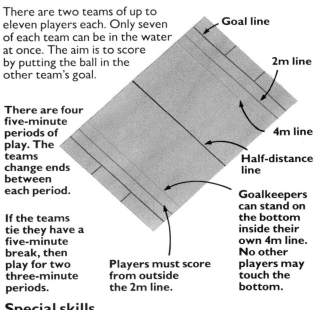

**Goal line**

**2m line**

**4m line**

**Half-distance line**

**Goalkeepers can stand on the bottom inside their own 4m line. No other players may touch the bottom.**

**Players must score from outside the 2m line.**

## Special skills

It is much harder to control a ball in water than on land. Use the tips below to help you.

**To pick up the ball, push it down. As it bobs up, put your hand under it and scoop it up.**

**Swing your arm back to cushion the ball as you catch it.**

**Keep your arm almost straight behind your shoulder to throw.**

## Goal!

★ Players can score with any part of their body.
★ At least two players must touch the ball before a goal is scored.
★ After a goal, the defending goalkeeper takes a goal throw from the goal line.

## Foul!

★ Physically obstructing an opponent is a major foul. The player leaves the water for 45 seconds or until a goal is scored.*
★ Using both hands to throw or catch, or pushing the ball under-water, are ordinary fouls, giving the other team a free throw.

### Free throws and corners

★ A free throw is taken if the ball goes out of the pool or hits the side and bounces back in. The opposing player nearest to where it went out takes the throw.
★ A corner is taken when a defender sends the ball over his or her own goal line. The attacking player nearest to where it went out takes the corner from the 2m line.

*After three major fouls a player is out of the game.

# Swimming kit

You need very little equipment for swimming, but there are all kinds of things you can use to make practising more interesting.

Below you can find out about the different swimming aids, and find advice on choosing swimwear that is right for you.

## Swimming trunks and costumes

Costumes and trunks come in a wide range of styles, patterns and materials; choose something that suits the type of swimming you do. There is quite a difference between fashion and racing swimwear, particularly for girls. Below are tips on what to buy for competitive swimming.

★ Look for swimwear from an established manufacturer, who understands what competitive swimmers need.
★ Check that the fabric doesn't absorb water or it will weigh you down. The material should be lightweight and stretchy.
★ Make sure it feels secure and fits snugly, without rubbing. If it is loose, pockets of resistance (see page 4) build up.
★ Check that it conforms with competition regulations.
★ Choose swimwear with strong seams: as you swim the fabric stretches, which puts pressure on them.

### Costumes only

★ Check that you can move your shoulders easily in any direction. Wide shoulder straps are more comfortable and less likely to roll.
★ Look for a high-cut neckline to improve your streamlining. Make sure it doesn't rub at your armpits or the sides of your chest, especially if you train over long distances.
★ Check that the legs, arms and neck are elasticated. The elastic should be covered with fabric and sewn in place to stop it moving about.

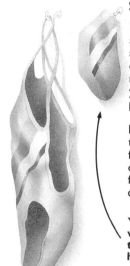

## Swimming caps

In some pools you are required to wear a cap. Make sure you check on the regulations before you go to a new pool.

If you have long hair it is a good idea to wear a cap, both for the benefit of other swimmers and for the people who clean the pool.

**Your cap needs to fit well, but if it is too tight it may cause headaches.**

## Flippers

Using flippers loosens and strengthens your ankles and allows you to make better use of your exercise time.

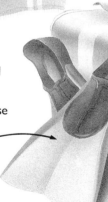

**Make sure your flippers fit well; if they are too big they can fall off and you also tire faster.**

# Floats

Floats vary in design and material, but they all allow you to stay afloat while isolating part of a stroke for practice. For example, you can grip the float between your legs and concentrate on improving your arm action.

If you plan to use floats regularly in training, it is worth buying a good quality one as the cheaper ones tend to break up quickly.

**Kickboards are large floats you hold on to while you practise leg actions.**

**Pullbuoys hold your legs in place and keep your body in the correct position while you exercise your arms. There are various sizes; choose one that feels comfortable.**

## Hand paddles

Using hand paddles is a good way to practise your arm action once you have a good stroke. The larger the paddle, the greater the effort you need to make.

**Choose a paddle big enough to exercise efficiently but not so big that you feel strained.**

# Accessories

Some people find the accessories below make swimming easier or more pleasant. It is really a matter of personal choice whether you use any of them or not.

## Goggles

Chlorinated pools and long training sessions can irritate your eyes, so most swimmers use goggles at least some of the time.

**Always take spares if you use goggles for racing.**

To avoid the eyepiece springing back into your eyes, make sure you put your goggles on correctly. First put the eyepiece on, then hold it in place while you stretch the strap over the back of your head.

## Ear plugs

To stop water getting in your ears, you can use plugs that mould to fit your ears exactly.

**Make sure you dry inside your ears properly after swimming.**

## Nose clips

**The plastic forms a 'U' shape when you press it over your nose.**

Nose clips are vital for synchronized swimming as some of the movements can force water up the nostrils. It is best to avoid using them in races as they can fall off quite easily.

33

# Getting fit

Swimming is good exercise but if you want to get really fit, the best way is to combine it with exercises on land.

Below is a warm-up routine to carry out before you exercise; opposite are strength exercises to improve your speed and stamina.

## Warm-up routine

The routine below loosens and gently stretches your muscles. This makes them less likely to strain and increases your suppleness. Do the routine slowly, stretching as far as you can but not more than feels comfortable.\* Hold all the stretches for six seconds, relax for six seconds, then repeat them.

Always warm down as well, using gentle exercises or a slow swim.

Press your head to the left, right, back and front. Repeat ten times.

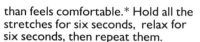

Sit with your legs straight and together, then 'walk' your fingers forwards. Repeat several times.

Swing one arm back then forwards ten times. Repeat with the other arm, then both together.

Sit with your legs apart. Extend one arm and stretch to the opposite knee. Repeat several times.

Put one arm over your shoulder and push the elbow down with the other. Do the same with the other arm and repeat several times.

Put one arm up your back, then the other. Link arms over your back and pull. Repeat several times.

With one leg straight and the other bent back, stretch forwards then lie back. Repeat several times and do the same the other way round.

Kneel down and interlock your fingers behind you. Bring your arms over in front of you. Repeat several times.

Sit upright, the soles of your feet together. Pull your feet up towards your body, then press your knees downwards. Repeat several times.

Extend one arm over your head and stretch to the side. Do the same the other way. Repeat several times.

Rotate each ankle clockwise ten times, then anti-clockwise ten times.

\*If you overstretch you can injure yourself (see pages 42-43)

# Strength exercises

You can build up your strength more quickly out of water than you can in it. These exercises will help you swim faster and keep going longer. Do each for 30 seconds, then rest for 30 seconds. If you feel any strain, particularly in your back, you should stop.

## Press-ups

Lie face-down, your hands palms-down beneath your shoulders. Push yourself up, with your back straight. Lower yourself nearly to the ground, then repeat.

**To protect your back, use a floor mat.**

## Sit-ups

Lie on your back with your knees bent and hands behind your head. Slowly lift your upper body and bring your head down towards your knees, keeping your feet on the ground.

## Squat thrusts

Crouch with your hands on the ground. Keep your hands fixed, then jump your feet backwards and forwards without stopping.

**Balance the chair against a wall for safety.**

## Step-ups

Quickly step up and down on to a low bench or chair, straightening your leading leg before stepping down. Vary which leg you lead with.

**Keep your legs straight.**

## Leg raise

Lie on your back and slowly lift your legs until they are at about 45° to the floor. Hold them there for a few seconds then slowly lower them.

# How your muscles work

Your muscles are made up of lots of fibres which shorten when you flex a muscle and lengthen when you relax. The fibres can be red or white.

**Red or slow-twitch fibre is good for slower distance work.**

**White or fast-twitch fibre is good for speed work.**

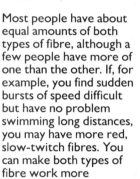

Most people have about equal amounts of both types of fibre, although a few people have more of one than the other. If, for example, you find sudden bursts of speed difficult but have no problem swimming long distances, you may have more red, slow-twitch fibres. You can make both types of fibre work more efficiently by training.

## Aching muscles

When you exercise, your muscles produce lactic acid which is carried away in the bloodstream as you exercise. If you stop suddenly it gets trapped in the muscles, delaying recovery. Warming up and down at the beginning and end of a swimming session helps avoid this.

# Training

If you enter competitions, it is vital to organize a balanced training programme. You can use the suggestions on these pages to help you get the most benefit from your swimming sessions.

## Organizing a training schedule

A schedule with the sections shown below helps you develop all-round ability and improve your fitness in specific areas. As a rough guide, spend half your time on endurance work, 40% on skills and drills and 10% on speed work.*

Reset button

Start-stop button

Using a stop-watch helps measure your improvement.

★ **Warm-up**. The length depends on age and weight: younger and lighter people need a shorter warm-up. For example, an average 11-year-old needs about 5 minutes but a hefty 17-year-old needs about 20 minutes.
★ **Endurance work**. This builds up stamina. You swim longer distances, say 400m to 1000m, with short rests of about 10 seconds between swims.
★ **Skills and drills**. You can organize these to develop specific skills and as a way to make your training more interesting.
★ **Main set**. This includes both endurance and speed work, in varying amounts, depending on your training needs at the time.

★ **Speed work**. You swim shorter distances with longer rests in between.
★ **Warm-down**. The same applies as for warm-ups.

### Sample schedule

Below are some ideas for the kind of things you can build into your training schedule.

★ **Warm-up**. 400m frontcrawl and backcrawl, alternate lengths of each.
★ **Endurance**. 1000m frontcrawl using bilateral breathing or 5 x 200m frontcrawl, 15-second rest between each 200m.
★ **Skills and drills**. 6 x 50m frontcrawl kick, 15-second rest between each 50m; or 6 x 50m frontcrawl, left arm and legs only on even numbers, right arm and legs only on odd numbers, 10-second rest between each 50m.
★ **Main set**. 4 x 100m breaststroke every 2 1/2 minutes (complete 100m then rest for the time that remains of that 2 1/2 minutes):
1st 100m: 2 legs kicks to 1 arm action.
2nd 100m: left arm only, right arm only, both arms, each action with a leg kick.
3rd 100m: 2 strokes on surface, 2 strokes underwater.
4th 100m: full stroke.
★ **Speed work**. 10 x 25m frontcrawl, 45-second rest between each 25m.
★ **Warm-down**. As for warm-up.

### Target times

You can use these targets to check your progress. Try timing yourself over the distances and see how your speed compares with the chart. After a few weeks, see if you can achieve the next stage.

| Stroke | Bronze 20m | Bronze 25m | Silver 20m | Silver 25m | Gold 20m | Gold 25m |
|---|---|---|---|---|---|---|
| Frontcrawl | 17.8 | 23.0 | 15.8 | 20.5 | 14.5 | 18.6 |
| Breaststroke | 21.6 | 27.8 | 19.9 | 25.6 | 18.1 | 23.3 |
| Backcrawl | 20.0 | 25.6 | 18.2 | 23.3 | 16.5 | 21.1 |
| Butterfly | 20.4 | 26.6 | 18.6 | 24.2 | 16.9 | 22.0 |

Times reproduced by permission of the ASA/ESSA.

### Training tips

★ Once you make a plan for a session, try to stick to it.
★ Don't set yourself impossible targets but aim for the highest goals you think you can achieve.
★ As you get fitter, try working hard at one session and not so hard at the next. Concentrate on your style during the easier session.

*Swimmers building up to competitions may vary these amounts slightly throughout the year according to their training needs.

# Training for competitions

Top swimmers spend months building up to competitions. Below are two training methods they use which you could include in your own training programme.

## Interval training

Interval training can greatly improve your performance. You complete either an endurance or speed swim over a set distance followed by a slow, active recovery or rest, then another swim, and so on. For example, you could swim 8 x 50m of your chosen stroke with a minute's recovery between each 50m.

As your fitness improves, you can make your training harder in several ways:

★ Allow yourself less recovery time so that you do the same work in less time.
★ Increase the distance of your swims.
★ Repeat the sequence more times.

## The 'taper period'

You need to capitalize on your months of hard training before a competition. It is a good idea to have a 'taper period' in which you train less but sharpen up specific race techniques. The taper period can be anything from a few days to several weeks, depending on what suits you.

On the right are suggestions for ways to train during the taper period so you hit the actual race day on peak form.

**Taper plan**

Have shorter and less frequent training sessions.

Practise starts and turns.

Do less endurance work. Concentrate on the race distance and race pace.

Rest more and sleep longer.

## Your heart and pulse rate

Your pulse rate shows how many times your heart beats per minute. When you train hard your heart beats faster than normal to pump more blood to your muscles.

Like any muscle, your heart strengthens with regular exercise. As it gets stronger it needs fewer beats to carry blood to your muscles.

Monitoring your resting pulse can be a good way to measure if your fitness is improving. Take your pulse with the least movement possible when you wake up. Try it again after a few weeks' training; you should find it is lower.

As you get fitter, training will feel easier and afterwards, your pulse will take less time to return to normal. To increase your fitness further you need to do more exercise – but don't overdo it.* Make sure you stop and rest if you feel tired.

### Taking your pulse

Place the middle fingers of one hand on the inside of your opposite wrist. To find your pulse, press your fingers down in different places until you feel a gentle throbbing.

Use a watch or clock with a second-hand and count how many beats you feel in fifteen seconds. To find your pulse rate per minute, multiply this by four.

*Your pulse rate should never go above around 180 beats per minute.

# Taking part in competitions

If you are about to take part in a competition, the tips on these pages will help you get the most out of the race day.

## The day before

★ Make a list of the things you need and pack them to avoid forgetting anything in the last-minute rush.
★ If you are swimming more than once, pack extra costumes and towels. It is uncomfortable to sit around in a wet costume between races.

★ Avoid eating rich or unusual meals the day before; they could upset your stomach. It is best to stick to familiar foods.
★ Keep your final training session light. You won't get any benefit from training hard at this stage and will only feel tired on competition day.

## Race day dos and don'ts

Do work out what you need to do before the race. Allow yourself plenty of time for each thing; panicking upsets your mental preparation and can easily be avoided by planning ahead.

Do check that you know exactly where the competition is being held and how to get there. Leave plenty of time for the journey.

Don't eat anything in the two or three hours before the competition, to allow time for digestion. On the race morning, eat easily digestible food like toast or cereal.

Don't have fizzy drinks, tea or coffee before or between races. If you feel thirsty, it is best to stick to water or fresh fruit juice instead.

## Thinking positively

If you approach a race feeling confident and positive, you are more likely to do well. Top swimmers use many of the methods below to get into the right frame of mind.

Set realistic training targets, such as improving your best time by a small amount. Achieving goals builds your confidence as you approach race day.

Plan a warm-up routine for the race that prepares you well without overtiring you. Practise your warm-up beforehand until it becomes automatic. On race day, the familiar routine should help calm your nerves.

Go through the race in your head: rehearse the pace and picture yourself swimming well. Imagine the sense of achievement as you cross the finishing line.

Try not to let butterflies in your stomach make you tense. They will go once you start swimming, and the adrenalin in your body which causes them will help you swim your best.

## Arriving at the competition

★ Report to the race officials and check the arrangements so you know what to do and where to go.
★ If there is a steward organizing each race, report to your race steward.
★ Don't just rely on other people to tell you what to do: sometimes there are last-minute changes to the race order, so listen out for any announcements.
★ If you have any problems, such as which lane you are to race in, stay calm and find an official who can help you.

## Pool layout

Below is a typical pool layout for a competition.

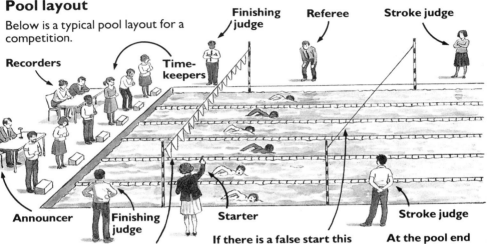

**Recorders**
**Time-keepers**
**Finishing judge**
**Referee**
**Stroke judge**

**Announcer**
**Finishing judge**
**Starter**
**Stroke judge**

**Flags five metres from each end above the water help backcrawlers judge their turns and finishes.**

**If there is a false start this rope is dropped and repeated starting signals or whistles are sounded.\***

**At the pool end a judge checks that swimmers turn correctly.**

| Before the race | Starting signals | After the race |
|---|---|---|
| ★ Change into your costume, ready for your warm-up.<br>★ If possible, finish your warm-up just before the start of your race. If you have to wait, stay as warm as you can by putting on a track suit. This prevents any muscle injuries and helps you swim your best. Have a land warm-up if you can't swim one.<br>★ Once your event is called, wait behind the starting block. | ★ A series of short blasts on a whistle means the race is about to start.<br>★ When you hear one long blast, take up your starting position at once.<br>★ You will then hear 'Take your marks'. When all competitors are still and ready the starting signal is given, either a blast on a whistle, a gun or klaxon, or 'Go'.<br>★ Inexperienced competitors can start in the water or dive from the side. | ★ Stay in your own lane until the referee asks you to leave.<br>★ Change into dry, warm clothes immediately afterwards.<br>★ Analyse how the race went, what you did well and what mistakes you made, and learn from both of them.<br>★ If you get a chance, thank the officials. They are usually volunteers who have given up their free time to be at the competition. |

*After three false starts the race goes ahead but competitors who started early are disqualified at the end.

# Olympic swimming and diving

An Olympic gold, silver or bronze medal is the major international award a top swimmer or diver can aim for. Below you can find out about how the Olympic swimming and diving events are organized.

## About the Olympics

★ The first record of Olympic Games being held dates back to 776BC, the time of the Ancient Greeks. They used sport as a way of keeping fit for warfare. The Games took place every four years until 393AD.

★ In 1896 the first modern Olympic Games were held in Athens, although it was not until 1904 that diving was recognized as an Olympic sport.

★ An international swimming body, Fédération Internationale de Natation Amateure (FINA), was founded in 1908 and laid down the rules for Olympic swimming events.

### Swimming events

**Freestyle**: 50m, 100m, 200m, 400m, 800m, 1500m
**Breaststroke, butterfly**: 50m, 100m, 200m
**Backstroke**: 50m, 100m, 200m
**Individual medley**: 200m, 400m
**Freestyle relay**: 4 x 100m, 4 x 200m
**Medley relay**: 4 x 100m

☆ **Record breaker**

Mark Spitz of the USA won a record seven swimming gold medals in the 1972 Olympics.

## Swimming heats

★ For each race, there are more competitors than places in the event. Heats are held to eliminate all but the fastest swimmers from the actual Olympic event.

★ The number of heats held depends on the number of entries from each country.

★ Each country can submit one competitor without him or her needing to reach the specified entry time. If the country enters more than one competitor, with a limit of three per country, each competitor swims in heats.

★ The heats are arranged to mix faster and slower swimmers. This is so that no swimmer can complain about being in a heat of slower swimmers while others were in more challenging heats.

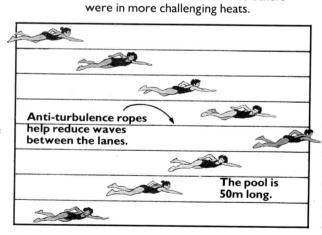

Anti-turbulence ropes help reduce waves between the lanes.

The pool is 50m long.

## The spearhead effect

The Olympic pool has eight lanes. The competitors' speed in the heats decides their race lanes. The swimmer with the fastest time is assigned to the lane right of centre. The other competitors are given the lanes alternately left and right in descending order of times, so that the slowest swimmers use the outside lanes.

If the entry times accurately reflect the swimmers' form, they should fan out into a spearhead shape during the race.

# Diving events

All dives are graded according to how hard they are. The maximum degree of difficulty for a dive is 3.5.

**Men's springboard**: five required dives (forward, backward, reverse, inward and forward dive with half-twist); six voluntary dives selected from five groups.

**Women's springboard**: five required dives as for men's springboard; five voluntary dives selected from five groups.
**Men's highboard**: four voluntary dives with maximum total degree of difficulty of 7.5; six voluntary dives without limit. Each dive is selected from a different group.
**Women's highboard**: four voluntary dives with

maximum total degree of difficulty of 7.5: four voluntary dives without limit. Each dive is from a different group.

## Preliminary contests

If there are more than 16 competitors, preliminary contests are held to decide which divers qualify for the event. For springboard events, the preliminary contest is eleven dives for men and ten for women. For the highboard, it is ten dives for men and eight for women.

Before preliminary contests, divers have to give complete written information about each of the dives they intend to do. These must be the same dives they will perform in the actual event. This is so the judges are prepared and know what to look out for.

## Scoring

Judges award marks from 0-10 to one decimal place for each dive. The highest and lowest marks are cancelled, the rest totalled. That figure is multiplied by the degree of difficulty to give a final score.

★ Dives other than those written down get no points.
★ Points are lost for restarting, losing balance, taking off to the side of the board or touching the end of the board during the dive.

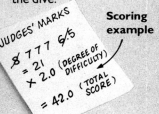

JUDGES' MARKS

8̸ 7 7 7 6̸ 5
= 21
× 2.0 (DEGREE OF DIFFICULTY)

= 42.0 (TOTAL SCORE)

**Scoring example**

# Diving boards

Springboards and highboards can be various heights, widths and depths. The ones shown here are used for Olympic diving.

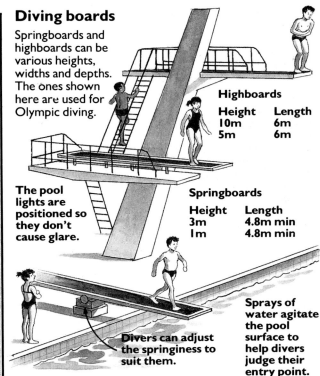

**The pool lights are positioned so they don't cause glare.**

**Highboards**

| Height | Length |
| --- | --- |
| 10m | 6m |
| 5m | 6m |

**Springboards**

| Height | Length |
| --- | --- |
| 3m | 4.8m min |
| 1m | 4.8m min |

**Divers can adjust the springiness to suit them.**

**Sprays of water agitate the pool surface to help divers judge their entry point.**

# Injuries

Swimmers tend not to suffer many injuries, but overtraining or concentrating too hard on one stroke can cause problems. If you feel any pain while swimming, stop; carrying on may make it worse. Consult your doctor for anything other than minor cuts and bruises.

## Shoulder problems

Backcrawl and butterfly swimmers are particularly vulnerable to shoulder problems. The symptoms can include pain at the top of the shoulders, difficulty in lifting your arms above your head and severe pain if you exert any pressure with your hand.

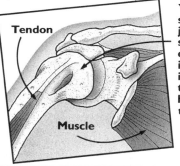

**Tendon**

**Muscle**

Your shoulder joint can suffer over-use injuries if you train too hard and too long.

## Knee problems

Kicking your legs puts strain on the ligaments which cross inside the knee joints. Breaststrokers should be especially careful not to devote too much training time to the stroke, although if you use the whip-like kick correctly you should minimize the risks to your knees.

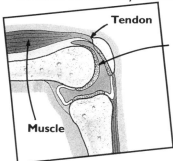

**Tendon**

**Muscle**

In frontcrawl or backcrawl, the cartilage may suffer through repeated kicking. This may make your knees buckle or lock.

## Home treatments

Strained and stiff muscles may be helped by the treatments below.

### Ice packs

Use an ice pack on the injury as soon as you can, as the cold helps reduce any swelling. To make an ice pack, put ice cubes in a plastic bag and wrap it in a towel.* Hold the pack on the injury for 15-20 minutes.

### Heat treatment

Heat applied to the injury later helps ease the pain and speeds up the healing process. Hold a hot-water bottle wrapped in a towel on the injury for 15-20 minutes. Hot baths and deep-heat creams from chemists also help.

## Avoiding injury

★ It is much easier to tear or strain a 'cold' muscle so make sure you warm up and warm down properly (see page 34).
★ Supplement your swimming with some land conditioning exercises (see page 35). Injuries happen if you put repeated strain on a part of your body that is not strong or flexible enough to cope.
★ Take an easy or rest day after a hard day's training.
★ If a limb feels strained when you swim, try changing its position slightly to one that feels more comfortable.
★ Balance your training between the different strokes.
★ Sometimes pain is from one stroke only; the cure may be to stop practising that stroke for a while.

*Don't use ice directly on your skin; it can give you a painful ice burn.

# How your joints work

Flexible joints and muscles help you avoid injuries. Your muscles help support your joints, and the stronger they are, the stronger your joints will be. If you don't keep supple, the muscles round your joints can eventually tighten up, which puts added pressure on the joints when you exercise.

To make your joints move, muscles pull on tendons connected to your bones. If you overstrain, your muscles pull too hard on your tendons and the connections may get damaged.

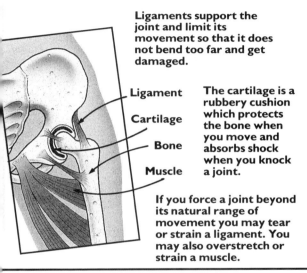

**Ligaments support the joint and limit its movement so that it does not bend too far and get damaged.**

**Ligament**

**Cartilage**

**Bone**

**Muscle**

**The cartilage is a rubbery cushion which protects the bone when you move and absorbs shock when you knock a joint.**

**If you force a joint beyond its natural range of movement you may tear or strain a ligament. You may also overstretch or strain a muscle.**

# Hypothermia

Hypothermia is a serious drop in core body temperature which can happen when you are cold, wet or exhausted. As you lose heat faster in water, it is a particular risk for swimmers. Below are some signs to watch out for.

- ★ Feeling cold
- ★ Shivering
- ★ Lips and fingernails turning blue
- ★ Slower reactions
- ★ Losing sense of direction
- ★ Blurred vision
- ★ Collapse
- ★ Unconsciousness

If you feel any of the early symptoms, get out of the water and dry yourself as quickly as possible. Don't rub your body to warm yourself up; you lose more heat this way. Wrap yourself in as many layers of clothing as you can and have a warm drink, like tea with sugar.

# Cramp

Cramp happens when a group of muscles suddenly contract. Straightening the cramped limb can ease the pain. It may be easier if someone else does this for you.

**Foot cramp**

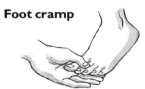

Straighten your toes by pushing them upwards, then stand on the ball of your foot.

**Calf cramp**

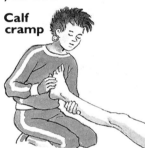

Straighten your knee, then pull your foot up towards your shin.

**Thigh cramp**

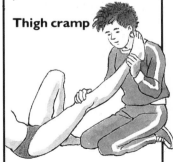

Straighten your knee, pull your leg up and forwards, then gently press your knee down.

# Life-saving

The most important life-saving measures you can take are learning to swim well and avoiding potentially dangerous situations. Even so, there could be a time when you find yourself, or someone else, in difficulties.

To take the basic life-saving knowledge below a stage further, try joining a life-saving course.*

## Getting into difficulty

Here are some of the most common problems you could face:

★ Falling into deep water and being unable to climb out.
★ Encountering strong currents.
★ Finding the weather conditions suddenly deteriorate.

★ Being cut off by an incoming tide and forced to swim for safety.
★ Not realizing how much shorter a distance you can swim in cold water. Even in summer, the temperature of open water can be over 10°C colder than it is in a swimming pool.

## What to do if you are in difficulty

If you find yourself in trouble, try to stay calm. Decide on your safest course of action: it may be simply to stay afloat until help comes, or you may have to swim for the shore. Below are some tips to help you in either situation.

### Keeping afloat

**Huddling together keeps you warmer.**

If you need to keep afloat for some time, aim to move as little as possible. Any exertion increases the flow of blood to your body's surface, where it is cooled by the water. This blood then circulates round your body and lowers your temperature, making you colder.

### Swimming to safety

Life-saving backstroke is good to use if you decide to swim for shore but have some distance to cover and are getting tired.

**Keep your body low in the water, with your knees below the surface.**

**Use a slow breaststroke kick and scull with your hands by your hips.**

### Treading water

To stay afloat in one place while using the minimum of energy, try treading water. Keep the action smooth and slow, with your body relaxed and upright.

**Hold your head just above the surface.**

**Pedal your legs slowly in circles as if you were riding a bicycle.**

**Press the water down and away from you with your arms.**

**You can use one arm to attract attention.**

*You can get details of courses from your local pool or library.*

# Rescuing other people

Anyone in difficulty is usually very frightened. You need to talk to the casualty all the time and explain exactly what you are doing, or about to do. If you can possibly avoid it, don't enter the water or touch the casualty. You put your own life seriously at risk – the casualty could panic and drag you in.

## Rescues from land

### Casualty nearby

★ Lie on the edge with your legs slightly apart. Hold on to something if you can or, if someone is with you, get them to hold your feet.
★ Reach out with a pole, stick or clothing. Get the casualty to hold it and pull him or her to the side.
★ If you have to get hold of the casualty yourself, grab the back of his or her wrist. If you grab the casualty's hand you could be pulled in.

### Casualty further out

★ If the casualty is too far away to reach, throw something that will help him or her to float, like a ball or lifebelt.
★ Try to aim the aid so it lands just in front of the casualty.
★ It is easier to be accurate with an underarm throw, but you may need to use an overarm throw for a longer distance.
★ Once the casualty has got hold of the aid, keep encouraging him or her to kick for the shore.

## Rescues from water

### Wading rescue

★ Take off shoes and heavy clothing and don't wade in further than chest-depth.
★ To get a firm grip on the bottom, lean back with your legs apart. Reach out to the casualty with a pole, stick or clothing.
★ If other people are around, link hands and try to form a chain out to the casualty.

### Swimming rescue

★ Undertaking a swimming rescue without training puts your life in real danger. If it is absolutely necessary, keep away from the casualty. Remember never to touch him or her if you can avoid it.
★ Reach out with a pole, stick or clothing. Get the casualty to hang on to it while you tow him or her back to the shore, swimming on your side.

# Glossary

**Aerobic** Energy system used when exercising, particularly in endurance work, to supply energy over a long time. It needs a good supply of oxygen.

**Anaerobic** Energy system used when exercising, particularly in sprinting, to supply a limited amount of energy quickly. It does not use atmospheric oxygen.

**Backcrawl** A stroke with a similar action to **frontcrawl**, but swum on the back. Popular with competitive **backstroke** swimmers.

**Backstroke** The name for any stroke swum on the back.

**Backward dive** A dive where the **take-off** is made facing the board and the diver continues backwards through the air.

**Belly flop** An incorrect dive where the diver's body smacks down flat on to the water. Usually caused by too high a head position during the **flight**.

**Bilateral breathing** Breathing alternately to the left and right at every third armstroke in **frontcrawl**.

**Body roll** In **frontcrawl** and **backcrawl**, a rolling movement used during the stroke to give the underwater part of your arm action more power.

**Bow wave** The 'wall' of water which forms in front of your head as you move through the water. It creates resistance but also provides a 'trough' behind the wave, which frontcrawlers breathe into.

**Breaststroke** A stroke swum on the front, where the arms work together, as do the legs, alternating with the arm action. Forms the basis for many life-saving strokes.

**Breathing** Moving air into and out of the lungs.

**Buoyancy** The way a person or object floats in water.

**Butterfly** A stroke where, like **breaststroke**, both arms and both legs work together. The legs kick together in a **frontcrawl**-type action.

**Catch** The point at which your hand starts to exert pressure on the water during the arm action.

**Density** How heavy an object is in relation to its size.

**Dog-paddle** A stroke swum on the front using a **frontcrawl** leg kick and an underwater 'paddling' action with each arm in turn.

**Entry** In swimming, the point at which your hand enters the water for its underwater stroke. In diving, the manner and shape you have as you enter the water.

**Flight** The part of a dive that takes place in the air.

**Freestyle** In competitions, a freestyle event is one where the swimmer can use any stroke; in practice, **frontcrawl** is usually used.

**Frontcrawl** The fastest of all competitive strokes, swum on the front. Each arm works alternately, one taking over from the other, with the legs also kicking alternately.

**Grab start** The most popular racing start. The push-off uses your hands as well as your feet. This gives you a quick dive off the block.

**Highboards** Rigid diving boards of various heights, used in advanced diving.

**Hurdle step** The final jump upwards and down on to the board before the **take-off** into a running jump or dive.

**Hypothermia** A drop in your body's core temperature, caused by being cold, wet or exhausted. It eventually stops organs, such as your heart and kidneys, from working.

**Inward dive** A dive where the **take-off** is made facing the board but the diver turns in the air, entering the water facing away from the board.

**Lactic acid** A by-product of exercise, which stops your muscles being able to contract, if produced in sufficient amounts.

**Mushroom float** A method of floating with the body curled into a ball, hands clasping your knees, so that your back just breaks the surface.

**Over-centre entry** In **frontcrawl** and **backcrawl**, reaching across the centre-line of your body when your hand enters the water.

**Oxygen debt** The amount of oxygen your body needs to reduce the **lactic acid** produced by **anaerobic** exercise.

**Pike** A diving position with the body bent at the hips and the legs straight.

**Pull** The movement of your arms during a stroke, ending at shoulder level, with the arms bent at the elbow.

**Push** The remainder of the arm action, continued after the **pull** and before **recovery**.

**Recovery** The final movement in the arm or leg action which returns the limb to the point from which it started.

**Reverse dive** A dive where the **take-off** is made facing forwards but the diver turns in the air, entering the water facing the board.

**Sculling** A propeller-like action of the hands and feet. It is often used when **treading water**.

**Springboards** Boards of various heights

and adjustable springiness, which give divers extra height at the **take-off**.

**Stroke cycle** A complete action of the arms and legs, in any stroke, which brings you back ready to start another cycle.

**Take-off** The point at which a diver leaves the board, block or side to dive into the water.

**Treading water** A way of staying afloat by moving your legs and hands.

**Underwater glide** An important glide to competitive swimmers as you travel faster underwater than on the surface. Used after racing starts and turns.

**Undulation** The unavoidable, but controllable, movements of your head, trunk and legs in **butterfly**, caused by the overwater arm **recovery**.

**Warm-down** A routine of gentle exercising used after training to help avoid aching muscles.

**Warm-up** Exercises used at the beginning of a training session to prepare your body and mind for more strenuous activity.

**Water resistance** The ways in which water acts against swimmers and slows them down.

**Whip kick** The most efficient **breaststroke** kick, as it combines low **water resistance** and a very propulsive leg action.

**Wide entry** In **frontcrawl** and **backcrawl**, entering your hand into the water outside the line of its own shoulder.

**Wind-up start** The fastest way to take over in a relay race. You build up momentum by circling your arms as you wait to take over. By stopping the arm movement as you dive, the momentum is transferred to your body and thrusts you forwards.

# Index

Photographs taken by **Simon Bruty, Jacques Cochin, Tony Duffy, Bob Martin** and **Mike Powell.**